This book belong

D0537429

....

Note to parents and carers

Read it yourself is a series of classic, traditional tales, written in a simple way to give children a confident and successful start to reading.

Each book is carefully structured to include many high-frequency words that are vital for first reading. The sentences on each page are supported closely by pictures to help with reading, and to offer lively details to talk about.

The books are graded into four levels that progressively introduce wider vocabulary and longer stories as a reader's ability grows.

Ideas for use

- Begin by looking through the book and talking about the pictures. Has your child heard this story before?

- Help her with any words she does not know, either by helping her to sound them out or supplying them yourself.

- Developing readers can be concentrating so hard on the words that they sometimes don't fully grasp the meaning of what they're reading. Answering the puzzle questions on pages 30 and 31 will help with understanding.

For more information and advice,
visit www.ladybird.com/readityourself

Level 2 is ideal for children who have received some reading instruction and can read short, simple sentences with help.

Special features:

Frequent repetition of main story words and phrases

Short, simple sentences

Large, clear type

Careful match between story and pictures

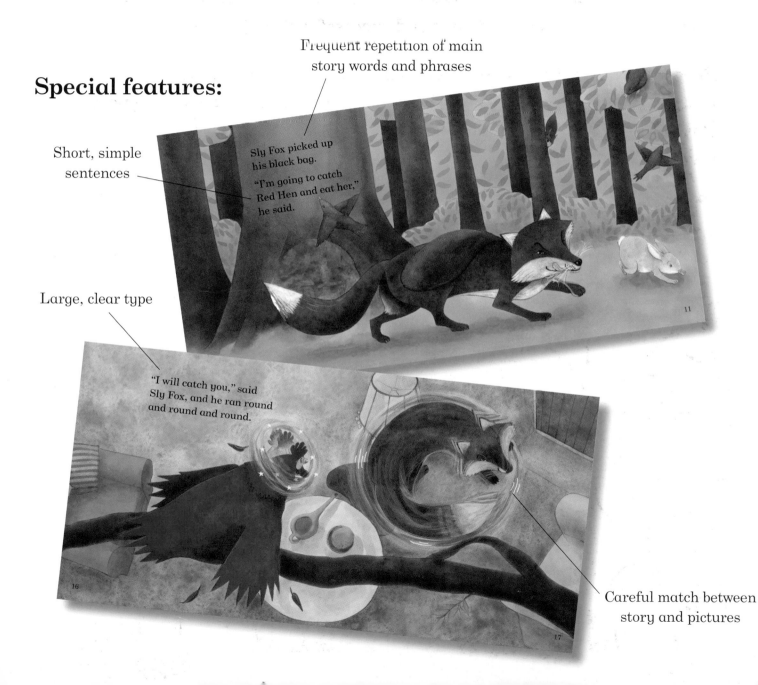

Sly Fox picked up his black bag.

"I'm going to catch Red Hen and eat her," he said.

11

"I will catch you," said Sly Fox, and he ran round and round and round.

16

17

Educational Consultant: Geraldine Taylor

A catalogue record for this book is available from the British Library

Published by Ladybird Books Ltd
80 Strand, London, WC2R 0RL
A Penguin Company

2 4 6 8 10 9 7 5 3 1
© LADYBIRD BOOKS LTD MMX

ISBN: 978-1-40930-356-5

Printed in China

Sly Fox
and Red Hen

Illustrated by Diana Mayo

Red Hen lived in a
little house in a tree.

Sly Fox lived in the wood.
And he was hungry.

Sly Fox picked up
his black bag.

"I'm going to catch
Red Hen and eat her,"
he said.

Sly Fox hid in Red Hen's little house.

"I'm the Fox, I'm the Fox, I'm really sly. You can't beat me, however you try!" said Sly Fox.

Red Hen saw Sly Fox and jumped up out of his way.

"You're the Fox, you're the Fox, you're really sly. But you won't catch me, however you try!" said Red Hen.

"I will catch you," said Sly Fox, and he ran round and round and round.

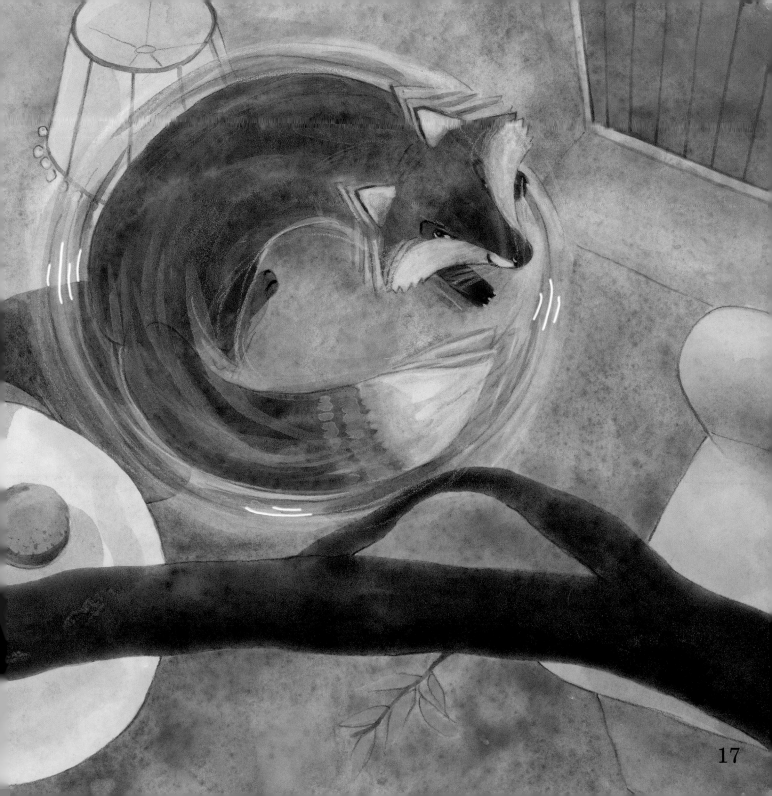

Red Hen's head went
round and round, too.
She fell down into
Sly Fox's big black bag.

19

Sly Fox ran into the wood.
The big black bag was
heavy, and Sly Fox sat
down to rest. Then he
fell asleep.

Red Hen jumped out of
the bag.

"You're the Fox, you're
the Fox, you're really sly.
But you won't catch me,
however you try!" said
Red Hen.

Red Hen put some
heavy stones in the bag.
Then she ran all the
way home.

Sly Fox tipped the bag into the cooking pot.

"I'm the Fox, I'm the Fox, I'm really sly. I will eat you. Say goodbye!"

The stones fell SPLASH!
into the hot water.

"Ouch!" said Sly Fox.
"I really hate that hen!"

How much do you remember about the story of Sly Fox and Red Hen? Answer these questions and find out!

- Where does Red Hen live?

- Where does Sly Fox live?

- How does Sly Fox catch Red Hen?

- What does Red Hen put in the bag?

Look at the pictures, then match them to the story words.

Red Hen

Sly Fox

stones

bag

wood

Read it yourself
with Ladybird

Read it yourself — Level 1 — The Three Billy Goats Gruff

Read it yourself — Level 1 — Cinderella

Read it yourself — Level 1 — Little Red Hen

Read it yourself — Level 1 — Goldilocks and the Three Bears

Read it yourself — Level 1 — The Magic Porridge Pot

Read it yourself — Level 1 — The Ugly Duckling

Read it yourself — Level 2 — The Gingerbread Man

Read it yourself — Level 2 — Sleeping Beauty

Read it yourself — Level 2 — Sly Fox and Red Hen

Read it yourself — Level 2 — The Three Little Pigs

Read it yourself — Level 2 — Town Mouse and Country Mouse

Read it yourself — Level 2 — Little Red Riding Hood

Read it yourself — Level 3 — The Elves and the Shoemaker

Read it yourself — Level 3 — Jack and the Beanstalk

Read it yourself — Level 4 — The Pied Piper of Hamelin

Read it yourself — Level 4 — The Wizard of Oz

Collect all the titles in the series.